BROKE

BROKE

A Poker Novel

BRANDON ADAMS

iUniverse Star
New York Lincoln Shanghai

Broke

A Poker Novel

iUniverse Star
an iUniverse, Inc. imprint

iUniverse books may be ordered through booksellers or by contacting:

iUniverse
2021 Pine Lake Road, Suite 100
Lincoln, NE 68512
www.iuniverse.com
1-800-Authors (1-800-288-4677)

Because of the dynamic nature of the Internet, any Web addresses
or links contained in this book may have changed
since publication and may no longer be valid.

This is a work of fiction. All of the characters, names, incidents, organizations,
and dialogue in this novel are either the products of the author's imagination
or are used fictitiously.

ISBN: 978-1-58348-471-5 (pbk)
ISBN: 978-0-595-88907-5 (ebk)

Printed in the United States of America

CHAPTER 1

THERE IS NO END
OF THE LINE

November 16, 2004
Vegas—Bellagio

"Go to room 6306."

Five minutes later, I arrive to find my friend Matt chain-smoking and absorbed in a couple of heads-up (one-on-one) poker games on Ultimate Bet (an online poker site). I can see by the hopeful way he's looking at the computer that he's stuck pretty seriously.

"How bad?" I say.

"Take a look." This comes from Rob, Matt's roommate and my best friend.

"Jesus."

Matt's opponent, Keyser, has $176,000 on one table and $230,000 on the other.

I watch in silence for a while; then Matt asks, "Raf, how much do you have on Ultimate Bet?"

This is not what I want to hear.

"Maybe forty," I reply. In truth, I have closer to $80,000 on that site.

"Send it." He might have added, *you owe me.*

It's true that Matt has loaned me money on many occasions, but in my mind these "loans" were strictly matters of convenience—times when he had cash on hand, and I didn't. There was never any serious danger that he wouldn't be paid back.

"Who do you owe?" I ask.

Rob speaks up, "Fifty to me."

"Thirty to Savage, twenty-five to Thompson," Matt adds.

So a total of $105,000 had been transferred to Matt's account, all on credit. I learn that another $54,000 had been sent over from Keyser's account, in exchange for the $54,000 in Matt's PokerStars account.

All eyes follow me as I log on. I send Matt $20,000. Usually regret follows a lag, but in this case, action and regret occur at more or less the same time.

I'm not getting the money back. I've seen this movie before. Matt is a smart guy and a talented poker player, but right now he's intent on taking things to the "end of the line." When a weekend gambler comes to Vegas and drops $600 in blackjack and then goes to the cage to get an advance on another $1,000, I can see his thoughts in his eyes: *This is it. If I lose this, I'm never gambling again. This is the end of the line.*

I want to tell him, "There is no end of the line. I've taken it to the end of the line many times and then figured out some way to take it further still."

"Matt, let's go grab a bite," I say.

"He'll be back in a minute."

"He's up two hundred thousand; you think he's taking off? Just write, 'Lunch. Thirty minutes.' He'll wait."

"No."

I think about kidnapping the computer or calling the hotel and telling them to shut off Internet access. Instead, I go to the neighboring room and make a couple of phone calls.

When I come back, Matt has lost another $18,000 and has reloaded with my money.

"Matt, I think you should pull the cord on this thing."

"Guys, just take off for a while. I can afford it."

My nerves are so raw that I honor his request. Rob and I walk around the deserted Bellagio pool, trying to take stock.

"How much does he have in the house?" We know that Matt's liquid assets minus his new debts amount to, at best, fifty grand. He had bought a new house in Vegas about six months ago.

"Maybe a hundred."

"How's he playing?"

"He's not thinking at all. He's smoked like five packs. He's totally fried."

"Any sleep?"

"None."

That means it has been at least two days.

"We need to kill it."

"Nope, can't do it."

This is a fairly predictable response from Rob. One of the many unhealthy features of the gambling life is that the gambler is not going to be saved from his self-destructive tendencies by other gamblers. It simply isn't done; free will is too highly valued.

"OK, I'm calling Tim and Will and telling them not to send him anything."

Tim and Will had lent money to and borrowed money from Matt in the past.

"What?" Rob protests.

"It's done," I say as I make the first call. It goes to voice mail. "Tim, it's Raf. Don't make any loans on Ultimate Bet today." I text message a similar request to Will.

"We need to get him walking around."

Right now, there is only one thing Matt is capable of: gambling. He can't sleep. He can't eat. He can't think. If we can get him walking around, the exhaustion and pain will gradually begin setting in.

"Not happening," Rob says.

"Fuck it," I say. "I'm taking the computer."

Fifteen minutes later, I'm looking at Matt's computer. He's up about $35,000 since we left.

I take a seat on the bed and watch in silence. Exhaustion and testosterone are displaying themselves in the form of absurd aggression. Thirty minutes later, he's up another $20,000. I need to sleep. I go to my room, take a hot shower and half an Ambien, and sleep for twelve hours.

I wake up at 7:15 AM, grab a coffee and a muffin, and head up to room 6306.

The first thing I notice is that Rob is drunk. Not a little bit drunk. More like what my brother would call "plow-assed." It isn't like ha-ha-fun drunk, either; it's more like I'm-going-to-kill-myself drunk.

Keyser has about $440,000 on two tables. I've seen everything online, and I've never seen a player with this much on one site.

Rob takes me aside. "He cleared my Stars account."

"How much?"

"Thirty-two."

This means that Rob sent the $32,000 he had on PokerStars to Keyser's account there, and Keyser in turn sent $32,000 to Matt's account at Ultimate Bet.

There's a long history of Matt staking Rob when he's broke or in debt. This makes the $50,000 Rob lent him earlier at least psychologically bearable. The additional $32,000 is triggering a mini-breakdown.

"OK, Matt, it's over." I start to shut the screen of his laptop.

"Get the fuck out of here."

I go to the bathroom, fill two glasses with cold water, and pour them directly on Matt's computer. In three minutes, it's fried. Had he promptly turned it off, he could have saved the computer, but of course, he played till the last second.

I take off for my room. No one stops me. The next day, I get a call from Matt. "I'm taking off for Chicago."

"Come up here first."

I give him two thousand in cash, and he's off. I call him a couple of days later.

"Let me call you back. I'm off to see a movie with my parents." As if nothing ever happened. Another day, another poker bust-out.

"Call me later, and I'll help you sort stuff out."

He never did.

CHAPTER 2

ADDICTION

November 22, 2004
Vegas—Palms

"This has to be the worst time in history to have a gambling problem." I'm at dinner with Rob, reflecting on Matt's unraveling about a week after the fact.

"I don't know. It depends how you look at it," Rob says.

"What do you mean?"

"OK, let's say you have a rat in a cage with his girlfriend rat, or whatever you want to call it. If you drop a new female rat in the cage, what's he going to do?"

"I don't know. Go to the new one, I guess."

"Hell yeah, he's going to go to the new one. Now let's say that you put a little electric fence right in the middle of the cage. You have our rat and the girlfriend rat on one side, and then you drop the new female on the other side. Now what happens?"

"Don't know. Depends how strong the charge is," I say.

"Nope, that's the thing; it doesn't depend. With no charge, of course he's over there, but they can pump that baby up to life-threatening charge, and he still makes the cross."

"OK, I think I see where this is going. Let me get this straight: even though the rat endured a near-fatal electrical charge to get to the new female, and even though he may have caused himself permanent physical harm … you're saying that, overall, this is a good thing for the rat."

"All I'm saying is the rat knows what he's getting into, and he decides it's worth it to make the cross. He had a choice. This isn't the worst time in the world to be a gambler. The worst time is when no one's gambling. What could be worse than always wanting to gamble and never having the opportunity?"

"If you stick cocaine in a rat's cage, he'll do it until he dies. Is that a good thing for the rat?"

"That's different. He doesn't know what he's getting into. If I hadn't seen fifty people destroy themselves on coke, I would have tried it and done it till it killed me. In the case of the fence, the rat knows from experience that the charge is going to be a little harsher next time around, and he still makes a go of it."

"The MRI of a gambling addict's brain while gambling looks nearly indistinguishable from the MRI of a coke addict's brain on coke. Both are pretty effective at shortcutting the pleasure circuitry. We're just a couple of addicts chasing dopamine jolts to the brain," I say.

"You're too pessimistic. Dopamine in the brain makes people happy. Name one activity where time passes faster than at the poker table. This is the best thing going. It just took the rest of the world a while to figure it out."

"OK, tell me that when you start running bad. Remember: they only call it a gambling problem when you're losing."

I've rediscovered my fascination with gambling addiction in the wake of Matt's bust-out. You can't be a poker player who doesn't think about addiction. It's like being an eighty-year-old who doesn't think about death. It's staring you in the face all the time.

I've seen the vicious circle of poker addiction so many times that I can outline it for you beat by beat. First comes the initial spark. For some people, this can be as simple as sitting down at a poker table for the first time. These are the genetically doomed; one sip and they are done. For others, the spark comes from a big win, a big loss, heated competition with poker/life rivals, or from larger life problems, like divorce, that require powerful distractions.

If a gambling addiction starts, the only thing that can prevent it from getting worse is personal agency, and, for most, this is not nearly sufficient. A gambling addiction attacks on two fronts. First and most insidiously, it destroys the attention span so that gambling becomes the only activity that can sustain the addict's attention for any length of time. Gambling stirs the brain chemicals in a way that few other activities can, and, increasingly, addicts find that gambling is the only thing they look forward to. If one has tendencies toward attention deficit disorder before one starts gambling, the probability of addiction is very high, because gambling for this type of individual is one of the few things that can focus the mind. Second, just as alcoholics cannot be satisfied by three shots, gamblers finds themselves constantly moving up in stakes. Bigger and bigger swings are necessary to generate the same gambling high.

Even for those who start with large bankrolls, a gambling addiction almost ensures financial ruin. In poker, one player's gain is another's loss, and as addicted poker players move up in stakes, it becomes more and more likely that the gain will be their opponent's, and the loss will be theirs. Further, the poker addicts often find themselves playing forty hours a week or more, which means that they will be paying more to the house in rakes and to dealers in tips than most people make in a year.

Like a golfer who has ingrained a flawed swing, the addicted poker player usually becomes somewhat ossified in his or her poker style. Learning ceases for the most part when one is in the throes of addiction. There always exists the intention to read and study the game, but, in part because of their damaged attention span, the gambler's only education occurs at the table.

Usually, poker bust-outs follow the Hemingway model: gradually, then suddenly. In Matt's case, it was just sudden. One day he was worth $300,000, and the next day he was $80,000 in the red. I find it especially hard to get my head around Matt's case because I always considered him to be a careful poker player. Most players would have picked Rob to go broke before Matt. Rob has always been cavalier about matters such as game selection and bankroll management; Matt had these things down to a science.

CHAPTER 3

THE PROFESSOR

November 24, 2004
Vegas—Bellagio

I'm sitting at the Bellagio $80/$160 hold 'em game, and out of the blue, Mason looks at me and poses a question.

"There are three logicians standing in a circle—Logician One, Two, and Three. Each of them has a positive integer written on his head. One of the numbers equals the sum of the other two. An observer comes by and says, 'Logician One, do you know what number you have written on your head?' Logician One doesn't know his number, nor do Logicians Two or Three, but when Logician One is asked a second time if he knows his number, he says, 'Yes, it's fifty.' What numbers do Logicians Two and Three have?"

Mason is an odd guy, and we've had similar exchanges before. In addition to being a top poker theorist, Mason is also a math professor at a third-tier university.

I go into deep-thinking, check-fold mode for about three minutes, then say, "twenty and thirty."

One guy at the table wants to know why that was the solution, and I tell him.[1]

"You haven't lost much, Kid," Mason says.

In truth, two years of late nights, drinking, and gambling have taken quite a toll, but I'm still a couple of steps ahead of most of the poker world. Mason happened to know that, in my late teens, I was a two-time Putnam Fellow, an honor bestowed on those who place in the top five in the nation's most prestigious collegiate math competition.

The poker world has a lot of very smart people in it. I've always found this odd because while poker is a complex game, it doesn't have the intellectual subtlety of, say, chess. I've often suspected that poker is more popular because of the huge chance element that comes into play. It allows fragile egos to attribute victories to skill and defeats to chance.

When I chat with intelligent people who are obsessed with poker, I sense that they feel that, at some point, their intellectual history went way off course, and now it is too late to correct it. The worst of these cases occurs when one's college life was largely devoted to poker. One finds more and more of these cases today. Once broke, poker addicts find that poker has rendered them largely unemployable.

---

1. Author's note: Explanation at end of text. The characters in *Broke* are composites of people I know in the poker world, and many of the scenes are based on my experiences. Raf is based, in part, on my friend Sasha Schwartz. Sasha did in fact solve this problem in three minutes while at the poker table. The physical equivalent of this feat would be something like a five foot vertical leap. I don't suggest working through this problem while reading the text.

To an outsider, I'm just another case of talent wasted on poker. As one of my friends likes to say, something is wrong when the best minds of our generation are calculating pot odds. I like to think that my case is unique, in that poker pulled me out of a deep hole instead of leading me into one.

*   *   *   *

The summer after my sophomore year at Harvard, I set out on a motorcycle trip from Milan to Barcelona with a close high school friend. Two hours into it, near the Italian-French border, I took a tight turn at too high a speed. The bike slid along the concrete for a short while before hitting the guardrail at over twenty miles per hour. The guardrail mangled my right leg. The doctors told me that after surgery and physical therapy, I'd be able to walk again, but I'd never be able to subject my leg to anything but the most modest forms of stress or impact.

Back at Harvard the next year, I replayed the accident in my head hundreds of times a day. I went through all of the particulars of the day and considered how altogether better my life would be if any little thread of the story had been different. Until I found poker, I was lost in a web of regret, unable to focus on anything for any length of time.

Following the typical pattern, my relationship with poker was a consuming one. Oddly, it represented a return to the academic way of thinking for me, rather than a departure. I approached poker as an academic discipline.

There are, in my view, four distinct levels to the game, and I sought to master all of them. Three of the four are firmly grounded in mathematics, while the fourth is more about psychology.

The first level is basic poker math, such as the probability of flopping two pair or the probability of ace-queen holding up against king-jack suited if both players are all-in before the flop. Also included in this level are basic odds calculations, such as the odds that a flopped straight will hold up against trips with two cards to come. Calculation of pot odds and implied odds would also be considered "basic poker math."

The second level involves understanding conditional probability as applied to poker. Bayesian statistics is the branch of mathematics that deals with proper updating given the introduction of new information. Many studies have shown that, in a variety of contexts, people are too slow to update their beliefs in the face of new information, and I, for one, can attest that there is no place where this is truer than at the poker table. Too often, one sees people lose huge amounts of money with pocket aces because they are unwilling to believe that the raises they face on the flop and on fourth street indicate that someone has improved to beat them.

The third level involves game theory, the science of interaction between thinking opponents. High-level poker is all about knowing how to vary your play in such a way as to always keep your opponents guessing. A recent magazine article that profiled online poker legend Erik Sagström, aka Erik123, focused on his phenomenal ability to remember past hands. In low-level play, this isn't a particularly important skill, but in high stakes games, a player's primary task is staying attuned for any type of predictability that might be exploited. Game theory provides the analytical basis for thinking about how to optimally mix up one's play.

The fourth level involves picking up "tells" on one's opponents. There are players, like Rob, who have an almost supernatural ability to read opponents' hands by taking cues from their body language. This is an area that I've gotten a lot better at over time, but it is surely the weak point of my game. Too often in the past, I've called a huge bet on the river because I picked up a "tell" on my opponent, then he turns over his cards and I think, *Oh, you've got the nuts. That's nice.*

*   *   *   *

I first met Rob at an undergrad game that was held at Harvard every Thursday in the basement of Winthrop House. It was a $3/$6 no-limit game, which seems quite small to me now but was at the time the biggest undergrad game offered. Rob was a Tufts senior who had been obsessed with poker since eighth grade.

I first played the game in late November 2001, during my senior year. I bought in for the minimum—$300. I was somewhat intimidated to see that Rob and Noah, a Harvard senior, each had at least $4,000 in front of them.

During my first hour at the game, Rob and Noah ended up all in on the turn with a board of six of diamonds, ten of hearts, two of hearts, and jack of diamonds (*6d-10h-2h-Jd*). They turned over their cards—Rob had a pair of jacks (*J-J*) for nuts, Noah had two tens (*10-10*). On the river came a ten (*10*). There was one card out of forty-four that could win the pot for Noah, and he had spiked it for over $8,000.

I was looking at Rob and thinking, *Don't you have a nervous breakdown at this point?* He seemed completely unfazed.

I asked him about it a few months later when we were on one of our frequent trips to Foxwoods, a hotel-casino in Ledyard, Connecticut. He said, "I might have looked unfazed, but that one hurt. Look, if you're a poker player, you've got to be able to take bad beats well. Here's the secret: When all the money's in, and everything is left to chance, tell yourself that you deserve to lose."

CHAPTER 4

MIXING VICES

February 18, 2005
L.A.—Commerce

Rob comes up to me and asks, "How's it going?"

I make a mental note never to ask anyone that question in the presence of possible clues that things are, in fact, not going well at all. Take a look, I want to say, notice the mountainous stacks in front of my three assorted opponents and the expanse of green felt in front of me, but I decide that Rob needs to be cut a break. Two months after the fact, he's still shaken by the eighty-two thousand that he's never getting back. Moreover, he has decided, for unknown reasons, to bring his girlfriend with him to Commerce tonight.

The two of them have seats at a $10/$20 no-limit game that's just a couple of tables away from my game, a $200/$400 hold 'em, Omaha Hi-Lo, and Stud Hi-Lo rotation game.

"Rob, listen to me. You're going to regret not playing a smaller game."

Rob defends himself, "No, look, I bought her in for the minimum and told her to go all in pre-flop with ace-ace, king-king, queen-queen, and ace-king. She's folding everything else."

People can justify anything. Rob, at this moment, is at the height of degeneracy. It's Thursday night, in perhaps the best place for going out in the United States, and he has decided to take his girlfriend to South Central L.A. to play poker. Worse still, rather than sit in a small game, where she might actually learn something, he has put her in a game where mid-four-figure swings are routine and given her a strategy that a six-year-old could execute.

"How long is the wait for three/six limit?" I ask.

"I don't know. At least forty-five minutes."

"It's worth it. Let me make a prediction—at some point in the night, one of you is going to lose a four-figure pot, and she's going to look like she's been kicked in the gut."

"Let's hope not," he says. "I've got to get back to her."

"Wait, one thing. How much did you buy in for?"

"Thirty," he says.

"Are you kidding me?"

"It's a deep game."

In any game where Rob figures himself to be the best player, he insists on being the biggest stack at the table, and apparently he sees no reason to change this policy in light of his girlfriend being present.

Rob doesn't realize that his absurdly high risk tolerance, developed over a long period of time, is almost certainly not shared by his girlfriend. Women are less inclined than men to think of money as a means of keeping score and are less likely to be fooled by the conversion of cash into chips.

Once I've convinced myself that Rob has no intention of leaving and that my game isn't particularly good, I decide to put my name down for a seat in Rob's game. Ten minutes later, I take a seat and buy in for $10,000. There's a lot of money on the table, probably the most I've ever seen at a $10/$20 no-limit table. Typically, the average stack size in such a game might be $3,000, but in this case it's closer to $9,000, and two players have over $20,000 in front of them.

Jessica, Rob's girlfriend, seems to be having a great time. She's having a lively conversation with the girlfriend of an Italian guy named Lorenzo, who's sitting in the game with about $25,000 in front of him. I hear the girlfriend mention to Jessica that Lorenzo plays all the time, which strikes me as odd because he makes a lot of extremely questionable plays, like opening the action pre-flop for $240 and betting $800 on the flop when there's only $250 in the pot. He seems to be a smart guy who thinks deeply about the game; it's just that the conclusions he has drawn regarding proper play differ from those that everyone else has settled on.

Jessica hasn't played a hand for the first hour and a half that I'm at the table. I can see the adrenaline start coursing through her as soon as she looks at her cards. The guy in fifth position raises to $70, and when Jessica goes all in for $320 more, he calls her. Jessica's kings hold up against ace-king suited, and she takes down the $820 pot.

Three hands later, Lorenzo opens the hand for $120 from under the gun (first to act) and has four callers, including Rob on the button. The flop brings *4s-6s-Jd*. Lorenzo checks; then Will, the player one to his left, bets $400. Rob calls; then Lorenzo raises to $1,500. Will and Rob both call. There is now $5,110 in the pot. Will is the third big stack at the table. He has about $15,000.

The turn brings the deuce of hearts. Lorenzo bets out $3,000, and Will and Rob both call. The pot is now $14,110. I think there is a fairly high probability that Lorenzo has made a set of jacks (three of a kind). He tends to alter the amount of his opening pre-flop raises based on his objectives in the hand. His $120 opening raise spoke of a hand that he wanted to get some action on but also wanted to protect. He thought that the board was unlikely to have hit anyone else, so he checked and risked giving the other players a free card. When Will bet out, and Rob called, Lorenzo likely figured that Will had hit his hand in some way and that Rob was on a flush draw, so when the bet came back around to him, he put in a decent-sized raise, but one that seemingly wanted a call. When both players called, he probably put Will on a set of fours or sixes, and Rob on a flush draw.

If I were him, I would have bet $5,100 after the deuce came, but he has settled on $3,000 as a satisfactory compromise between his competing desires to protect his hand and to extract the maximum with what was, on the turn, almost certainly the best hand.

The fifth community card is going to confront Lorenzo with an interesting situation. He will be first to act, which means that his opponents will glean some information from the time that it takes him to act. That said, regardless of what card comes, he is going to be faced with a difficult decision that will warrant a sizable allocation of time.

The river brings *8c.*

I look over at Jessica's neck and notice that her pulse is extremely rapid, seemingly dangerously so. I also notice a dejected look in Will's face that indicates to me that he has ace-king of spades. I'm rarely able to pick up a read on Rob, but I picked up on a slight adrenaline surge, and his hole cards became fully apparent to me.

Lorenzo looks extremely wired. It isn't clear to me that he's picked up on the fact that Will has missed his draw. He makes a quick glance at Will's and Rob's respective stacks, and says with little hesitation, "I'm all in."

Will throws his hand in, then Lorenzo's face evidences in quick succession surprise as Rob says "call," then delight as Lorenzo considers the idea that Rob has the lower set, and then shock as Rob turns over *5d-7d.*

Lorenzo had been inflexible in his read of the hand. He had put Rob on a flush draw and Will on a set. He'd thought that if he went all in, Rob would fold, and Will would call for his remaining $11,000 or so.

By going all in, he'd avoided the practical difficulties of counting the pot and Will's stack when his pulse was 180, but he'd also given up his option to fold if he bet enough to put Will all in and was then raised by Rob. Lorenzo mentioned later that it really didn't matter that he'd gone all in rather than betting a smaller amount, because if he had bet $11,000 and was then raised $9,500 more by Rob, he would have called.

Despite the fact that Rob dragged a $55,110 pot, Jessica wears a pained expression on her face for the next thirty minutes. She doesn't seem aware of the fact that she was upset; it's more like her mind is rapidly thinking through the events of the past hour, and her face is reflecting the fact that not all the thoughts are pleasant.

Lorenzo's girlfriend, on the other hand, would hardly need to be told that she looks upset. She glances at Lorenzo, first with incomprehension and then with contempt as he pulls three $5,000 chips from his pocket and resumes playing. She doesn't say a word to Jessica now that Rob has dragged $25,110 of her boyfriend's money to his side of the table.

In spite of the fact that Lorenzo's $15,000 is probably going to be a bit more active than it should be, Rob decides it is time to leave.

Later that night, Jessica tells him that he can play all he wants, but she is never going to step foot in a poker room again.

CHAPTER 5

THE SICKNESS

March 3, 2005, morning
L.A.—Lost Canyons

Today is golf day. The track is the Shadow Course at Lost Canyons. It's only an hour's drive from downtown, but it seems remote enough to be a nuclear weapons testing site.

"I'll bet you five hundred that I can hit it over that mountain," Rob says, demonstrating either some kind of severe depth-perception problem or an acute need for action.

Rob is the best golfer in the group. I manage to shoot around one hundred ten despite my weak leg. Antoine, a poker friend of Rob's and the third member of our threesome, hovers around ninety.

"I'll take it, and I'll give you two-to-one," Antoine says.

I'm mystified as to why Rob thinks he will be able to hit the ball over the mountain in question. It's obvious to me that the crest of the mountain is at least three hundred yards away and eight stories high. The urge to gamble must come from the more primal areas of the brain because, over and over again, I've seen it overcome every rational sense.

Rob implicitly accepts Antoine's offer by teeing up the ball and aiming in the direction of the mountain. He takes a vicious cut at the ball. The ball comes off the club with impressive velocity; it can be heard tearing through the air in the initial moments after impact. I think for a short moment that it's my depth perception that's off.

When the ball comes to rest, it's clear that the mountain top is much, much farther away than any of us had guessed.

"I can't believe you can fool your mind like that," I say.

"Dude. You missed that by like six hundred yards," Antoine follows.

*   *   *   *

In poker, one must constantly fight the mind's deep drive to gamble. I've always found it funny that people tend to change the read they have on their opponents so as to fit their need to gamble.

For instance, say you raise in a shorthanded game (one with six players or less) with *A-4* and get two callers. The flop is *Q-J-4*. You call; then the turn comes up *A*. At this point, there is a strong psychological tendency to change your beliefs about your opponent's hand. Specifically, you will now convince yourself that he or she has a very strong hand but one that is weaker than yours, something like *K-Q* or *Q-J*. People tend to change their reads on their opponents in order to ensure a continuation of heavy action.

*   *   *   *

"It's OK. I've still got you guys by a couple of thousand."

This much is true. Rob always seems to win the betting on the first tee. This is odd because he surely has the most acute need for action.

"Yeah, but by the looks of it, you're down a lot more than that in basketball," Antoine says. He's thumbing through scores on his cell phone.

My test for sports gambling degeneracy is whether you will bet on sporting events without watching them. Rob is failing that test miserably today. He's laid down bets on at least fifteen different college basketball games, most of which will be going on while we are golfing. His record on betting sports is not good; as in poker, the house take kills almost everyone in the end.

"It's OK. I'll make it up tonight." Rob is referring to tonight's fight between Bernard Hopkins and Felix Trinidad.

"How much do you have on it?" I ask.

"Twenty thousand to win five," he says.

That meant that Hopkins was a four to one favorite.

"Rob, that's idiotic. That's a thousand bucks in juice for something you have no edge on," I say.

"The boxing analyst from TheFightReport.com says that Hopkins is at least a ninety percent favorite."

People love to overweight small kernels of information in this way.

"You're never going to believe who's going to be there," Rob adds.

"I thought you weren't going to tell him," Antoine says.

"I wasn't, but fuck it. Matt's back."

"He's living in L.A.?" I ask.

"He's just visiting this week. He's moving out in about ten days. He's subleasing a room in Santa Monica."

"How's the bankroll?" I ask.

"I'll let him give you the details. Basically, he's played some-thing like twelve thousand hundred-dollar sit'n goes on Party Poker since we last saw him. He says he's up eighty thousand."

"A debtor who says he's up. That's a new one. Is he going to pay you?"

"Yeah, forty thousand in ten days, then the remaining forty-two over the next few months. I couldn't believe it when he told me. He said that he had decided that he wasn't going to tell me anything until he played ten thousand sit'n goes. It was like a mission for him. He played six tables at a time, all day, every day, starting some time in January. I wish he had told me earlier."

March 3, 2005, evening
Rob's house—Hopkins v. Trinidad

I arrive for the fight at the start of the third round. I take a seat next to Matt.

"You have any money on this?" I ask. This seems like a rea-sonable way to reacquaint ourselves. I know that Matt would like to slip into his old life with as little discomfort as possible.

"Nothing," Matt replies.

"That's a first."

Matt isn't a crazy sports gambler, but he would always put a couple of hundred on an event if he was into it, and a couple of thousand if it was a boxing match.

"Yeah, I'm a bit more careful these days. I'm sure Rob told you. Been grinding it out in Party sit 'n goes. Nothing else."

I have the brief thought that playing six games at once, all day, every day, has destroyed Matt's attention span to an extent that he can no longer be bothered with constructing fully formed sentences.

"Do you think Trinidad has a chance?" I ask.

"He took the first two rounds."

This explains the unblinking, uncomprehending stare that Rob is directing toward the screen. I have never associated a "look" with high blood pressure before seeing him at this moment. Rob is usually a calm guy.

"He's not the only nervous gambler out there," I note. The Vegas line dictated that anyone betting on Hopkins had to lay heavy odds; the general view was that Trinidad was past his prime. Picking Hopkins entailed wagering a lot to win a little.

The money involved in all aspects of boxing—from the amounts wagered to the amounts paid for TV access to the amounts paid to the boxers themselves—seems at times to trump the money involved in any other sport.

People like to watch other people in high-risk situations. On television, one, two, and three in ratings among "sports" are football, car racing, and poker.

The commentators give Trinidad the third round as well. The television judges disagree about the fourth round. The HBO cameras cut to the two fighters in their corners as they prepare for the fifth round. Trinidad bears a look of seriousness and determination; Hopkins flashes a quick smile to the cameras.

From this point, the fight unfolds like a chess match between slightly unequal opponents, a tale of slowly accumulating advantages revealing themselves in increasingly visible manifestations of dominance. Hopkins demonstrates none of the mercy that was characteristic of the only man of his weight to consistently outclass him—the inestimable Roy Jones Jr.

The referee stops the fight just before the start of the eleventh round.

Rob is glowing. The win of $5,000 is unremarkable by his standards, but it represents a swing of $25,000 from what the probable outcome was at the start of round four.

"Round up, boys, we're going to Cabana," Rob says.

Antonio, Matt, and I do as we are told and go with him. On the way to the club, Rob makes no fewer than ten calls, congratulating himself on the fight and inviting everyone to his table at the Cabana Club.

March 3, 2005, late night
Cabana Club

The key to garnering respect in the L.A. social scene is the same as the key to garnering respect in the poker world. You must actively court destruction without allowing it to take you down.

A friend of Rob's closes the curtain to our cabana, and half the group does lines of coke. The closing of the curtain is gratuitous because, in L.A., doing coke in the open is not that unusual.

It's no wonder that many of the world's best poker players make L.A. their home. The culture is very conducive to poker. Playing poker entails doing nothing productive whatsoever; in L.A., this is not considered such a bad thing.

I didn't know that Rob did coke, even on occasion, until this moment. Relative to the others, he seems to take in the drug expertly and in quantity.

Matt is smoking cigarettes and drinking Coke. Matt rarely drinks alcohol and never does illicit drugs. He is a purist as far as addiction is concerned. He simply needs speed. Give him caffeine, nicotine, and gambling, all in unhealthy quantities.

Having observed Matt today, my sense is that he has, at least temporarily, killed the gambling beast inside of him. By virtue of doing that, he has become a grinder, one of the uncool of the poker world. People are never going to love the guy who grinds it out in the $20/$40 limit game. They want the guy who, for better or worse, takes his chances.

CHAPTER 6

THE EGO HAS LANDED

March 15, 2005
San Jose—Bay 101

Male ego is the chief engine of ruin in the poker world. A poker table seems like an absurd venue for a clash of egos, because in any given game, the role of chance far overwhelms the role of skill. I've always considered myself more immune than most to the ruinous aspects of ego. For that reason, it can be considered surprising that I'm finding myself in a heads-up, $400/$800 limit hold 'em match against an opponent I know nothing about.

The genesis of this match is strange.

*   *   *   *

I was playing $100/$200 hold 'em at the Lucky Chances in San Francisco with a good friend named Luis. He had entered a hand in early position with a raise with, as it turned out, king-four suited (clubs). He'd been called by a woman named Jean, two seats to his left, as well as two others. The flop came

Ac-10c-7h, with two clubs. It had been bet and raised four times for a five-bet, and three players had stayed in. A club had come on fourth street. Jean had bet, and Luis had raised. Jean had called and then folded to a bet on fifth street.

Luis had shown his hand (the nut flush). Jean then said, "I put you on king-four of clubs."

This had struck me as one of the most ridiculous statements I've heard at a poker table. When someone enters a pot in early position, king-four suited is one of the last hands you put him on, and this is particularly true in the case of Luis.

I'm usually a gentleman at the table, so it had been a break in character when I'd said to Jean sarcastically, "You put him on king-four of clubs."

She'd said, "Yeah, I can always put people on a hand."

Her method for doing this, apparently, was mystical rather than deductive.

Partly because of a wounded ego and partly because I'd smelled blood, I had challenged Jean to a heads-up match. The floor would not let us break a full game to play heads up unless we wanted to play bigger than the game at hand. The dealer had said that he could only start a new game if we wanted to play $400/$800.

That's a bit higher than I'm comfortable with for heads-up play, but, given my desire to avenge Jean's personal effrontery, I had agreed.

What followed is an exquisite form of psychological torture.

*   *   *   *

Jean is, I imagine, the worst player to ever play $400/$800 heads up and also the luckiest. Heads-up limit is my game of choice. Against someone who plays as badly as Jean, in live play, my advantage should be about three big bets an hour, or $2,400. Of course, in any given session, even a fairly long one, the results will be primarily determined by chance, and, in this particular session, I lose $55,000. We play for five and a half hours, often to a large audience. In terms of damage to bankroll, ego, and reputation, this was a heads-up match without precedent in my poker life.

Given my skill advantage, it would have been wise for me to play Jean heads up for as long as humanly possible. As it turns out, I'm the one to throw in the towel, mostly because I feel a vein palpitating on the side of my head, suggesting the possibility that this match is destroying my health, along with everything else in my poker life.

I would have played her the following day and every day thereafter, but she left for San Diego, where she claims she's a successful Internet player. In heads-up play, she has an obvious and exploitable error, which is to almost always slow play big pairs while betting draws hard, which is about as bad a strategy as you can come up with when consistently applied.

The vein palpitation continues intermittently when I get back to my hotel room. A lot of poker players seem to have veins sticking out on their foreheads. I hope I won't get one of these.

Assuming that the palpitation has something to do with blood pressure, I take ten milligrams of propranolol, a beta blocker. Cosmetic pharmacology has reached an advanced level in the poker world, and occasional use of propranolol is my one concession to the trend. Beta blockers are taken by actors and other performers to lower blood pressure and generally reduce the physiological consequences of nervousness. Poker players take them for the same reason. After all, a slight shaking of the hand as a player moves his chips (the most reliable tell in poker) can cost him or her thousands of dollars

There is an online player on PokerStars who goes by the screen name "Zoloft." This is a play on the fact that antidepressant use among gamblers runs high. The causality isn't clear, but one interpretation is that the constant chemical assault that is gambling causes the body's sensitive adrenal system to go a bit haywire, and antidepressants are needed to bring it under control.

Xanax is commonly used to ease the nerves after bad sessions. Serious poker is not conducive to sleep, and many players have to take Ambien to get to sleep after an intense session. That old standby, marijuana, is also used by more than a handful of poker players. Serious non-pros are known to fuel thirty-six hour poker sessions with cocaine. All this suggests that poker is, on the whole, extremely damaging to health.

Serious exercise offers stress reduction to the poker player, but the offer is seldom taken up. This lack of exercise, when coupled with casino food, bad posture, and sitting in place for long periods of time, is capable of producing some extremely unattractive figures. I stay in decent shape through swimming, but most pools are closed when I need them most—late at night, after a stressful poker session.

I haven't done any research on twitches, but, anecdotally, it seems that the incidence of serious twitches in the poker world is exceedingly high. The fear of developing a disfiguring twitch has ended more than a few of my poker sessions. The mechanism by which poker stress translates into a permanent twitch has always been mysterious to me, but I'm pretty sure it exists.

There is one drug that people slow down on when they start poker—nicotine. Apparently poker is more addictive than cigarettes. Most poker rooms are nonsmoking, and it is not uncommon for two-pack-a-day smokers to go three hours without a cigarette while playing.

CHAPTER 7

THIRTY HOURS UNDERGROUND

March 20, 2005
New York

Internet poker is a highly addictive activity, maybe the single most addictive activity that I've ever encountered. It is also highly forgettable. Precious few of the hundreds of hours that I've spent online have stuck in my memory.

The same cannot be said for live poker, especially live poker that takes place in shady places. The characters that you meet at, say, the Players' Club in New York or the Casino Europa in Costa Rica have a special tendency to stick in the memory.

The New York underground poker scene is not quite as thriving as one might expect it to be. Hours wasted weigh more heavily on the psyche in New York than they do in L.A. or Las Vegas. There is an undercurrent of ambition in New York that prevents people from wasting an afternoon at the card table without guilt. Vegas depends on such wasted afternoons, and much thought has gone into designing the city's environment in such a way that one can blow through one's money and time without compunction. In L.A., everyone seems to be in a perpetual state of planning, so a wasted afternoon does not make one feel like he or she has fallen very far behind.

It's 4:00 AM on Thursday morning, and Rob and I have been playing poker since 2:00 AM on Wednesday morning. I doubt if anyone has ever set out to play twenty-six consecutive hours of poker. At some point, you find that you're not in good enough mental shape to do anything but play poker. Even simple things like walking across the street to get a hot dog are beyond you. You don't feel like going to sleep either, so you just stay and play poker. The next thing you know, you've been playing for twenty-six hours.

There are some things you should keep in mind when playing in an underground club. First, they're called "underground" because it's illegal to run a game that takes a rake unless you're in a city where gambling is legal, and you have a license. Second, underground poker games in various cities have historically been subject to armed robbery; this is a natural consequence of the fact that poker involves large sums of cash. Third, the people who are playing with you are at least vaguely aware of these facts and have decided to play anyway.

Neither Rob nor I have a lot of experience playing in shady places, but I'm beginning to think that I have a better intuitive feel for this stuff than he does. During a poker game, one shouldn't have to calculate things such as, "the probability that the guy in seat ten will kick my ass," but my sense at the moment is that Rob should divert most of his mental energy to this question.

Seat Ten is an unattractive personality. A fat man, a smoker, and an obviously degenerate gambler, he seems to be an absolute glutton for every form of weakness. This makes him a far from remarkable character in the world of 4:00 AM underground poker. What makes him unique is that he seems to have a penchant for inflicting punishment on people other than himself.

I learn of this from a guy named Tommy, who's seated immediately to my right. "That guy is going to get himself killed," he says of Seat Ten.

"Why is that?"

"If he's drunk and losing, he'll sometimes follow people outside and take the money back," he says.

"Why haven't they kicked him out?"

"They don't know about it," he replies. That seems unlikely but possible. When Tommy said that Seat Ten was going to "get himself killed," he was alluding to the common belief that the club was associated with organized crime, but on a day-to-day basis, the club was run by a rotating cast of shady twenty-somethings who seemed to stay focused on the fundamentals of money coming in and money going out and were not overly concerned with details such as whether customers were getting beaten up a few blocks away.

I cease conversation with Tommy. I'm preoccupied by an alarming change in my hearing, as if, all of the sudden, the clanking of chips has become twenty decibels louder. After about ten minutes, Seat Ten gets up, and Tommy says, "Your friend should take off while he's in the bathroom."

I walk across the table to seat five and relay this message via whisper to Rob.

"No, you can go. I'm staying till eight, at least. Look, I know the guy is pissed, but he's going to be less pissed at eight than he is now, and he might leave before then."

Seat Ten was "pissed" for the normal reasons; he was the victim of some admittedly horrendous beats at the hand of Rob. In addition, Rob didn't like the guy and would occasionally throw out barbs like, "Shit, sorry about that. I was hoping you wouldn't call"—a totally inappropriate thing under any circumstance, but especially after you bluff all in on the turn with a gut shot and hit.

The rule is simple: the worse the beat, the less you say. Once, late in a tournament, I ended up all in on the flop with an ace of clubs and a king of diamonds on a board of king of spades, six of spades, and two of hearts. The other guy had a set of sixes. A king came on the turn, and an ace came on the river. What could I possibly say to that guy that's going to make him feel better?

At about 6:00 AM, the hearing thing starts to scare me, and I tell Rob that I'm taking off. "Wait a sec. I'll go with you," he says. Seat Ten follows us outside and walks with us to Third Avenue.

The three of us stand next to each other in silence as Rob and I flag a cab. It seems to me that he's not going to do anything; he's standing there to intimidate us. We successfully flag a cab and hop in without incident.

Rob tells the driver, "Fiftieth and Eighth," but before the driver takes off, Seat Ten opens the door and makes a seat for himself next to Rob.

The driver says, "Is he with you?"

I say, "No."

Seat Ten says, more firmly, "I'm with them. Go."

The cab driver takes off. His calculus seems to be that while this is not a good outcome for the two young guys in the back seat, it's for sure his lowest-risk option.

The three of us get dropped off at the corner of Fiftieth and Eighth, only steps from Rob's apartment.

"Look, I'm going to make it easy on you guys. Stake me for five thousand. I'll give you half of what I win in the next week."

"I'm in debt. I can stake you for five hundred," Rob says.

"Twenty-five and we're done."

"How about a grand?" I say.

"Fine. Don't ever sit at my game again."

With that, I peel off ten hundreds, and Seat Ten takes off.

In the elevator, Rob counts out $1,000 to pay me, and says, "The degenerate and unskilled."

That summed up Seat Ten perfectly—he was a guy who would do anything for his next buy-in. He probably calculated correctly that the worst that would happen to him at the club would be that he wouldn't be able to return.

"Think we should call the cops?" I ask.

"No, they're not going to do anything. I'll e-mail the club about it anonymously."

CHAPTER 8

BLOWING UP

March 23, 2005, 5:30 AM
New York—Port Authority Bus Terminal

I'm having one of those what-am-I-doing-with-my-life moments. Any doubts that you have about whether you've taken the right path in life are likely to surface at the Port Authority Bus Terminal. In a spectacular display of degeneracy, Rob and I had decided that instead of leaving for Atlantic City on Friday night as planned, we would wake up at 5:30 AM on Tuesday and get there in time for that day's tournament.

At some point on this bus trip, I'm planning to broach a topic that Rob will find, at a minimum, extremely grating. I pretend to read *I Am Charlotte Simmons* while I think about how I could politely discuss what dearly needs to be discussed. Unable to find an elegant solution, I just come out with it.

"I went through your trading account while you were at the gym the other day. It's not pretty."

"What? How?"

"I saw your trading notebook next to my computer, and I couldn't help myself."

In the time it takes me to offer this excuse, Rob no doubt figures out how I got into his account. We both keep almost all our money at Charles Schwab. The default user name is the client's Social Security number. We have each other's Social Security numbers because we traded action on a few different tournaments last year and had to make note of this fact on our tax forms. His password was the same one that he uses on PokerStars. He'd given me this password a month ago so that I could log in and finish a tournament for him when his Internet connection went out.

"I told you that I lost a hundred and twenty grand messing around with options. That wasn't a warning?" I continue.

Poker teaches you to handle the loss of a large amount of money in a short amount of time with equanimity. When the risk tolerance of a poker player meets the explosive leverage offered by financial derivatives, the result is frequently complete destruction of the portfolio.

I had no idea how much Rob had had before I looked at his account. Poker players find it important to project a winning persona at all times, even to their close friends. Rob had won two of the twenty biggest online tournaments held in 2004, and he'd fared very well in cash games. All told, I had guessed that his bankroll was about $750,000 in October, which was a couple hundred thousand north of mine at that time.

"Are you really down to eighty thousand?"

"I've got twenty thousand in Bellagio chips, but other than that … yeah, that's pretty much it."

Shamefully, once I had logged into his account, I was like a married guy in Costa Rica who, upon deciding that he's going to take a hooker to his room, decides that he might as well take six. I combed through the "history" section of his account and learned exactly how he had lost his money.

"I've got the broad outlines. What was the XGenTech stuff?"
He seemed to have lost about $250,000 on a company I'd never heard off.

"Stupid. Linden turned me onto it. I just convinced myself that it was a sure thing."

"Rob, Linden's a degenerate."

Linden's a guy who's always floating around the big poker tournaments. I've always thought that he was a hopeless, near-broke gambling addict, but he always tries to convey the impression that he's the consummate Wall Street insider, and apparently Rob believed him.

"Yeah, I don't think we'll be seeing him around anymore. XGen broke him."

"Why'd Linden like the trade? What does he know about clinical trials?"

"Well, Linden sent me a spreadsheet from a hedge fund guy he knew who tried to estimate value given that XGen's new drug was approved and given that it wasn't approved. This guy estimated that the market was assuming that there was only about a 20 percent chance of favorable data. Linden said that this guy had told him privately that his firm had spent more time and money researching the trial than anyone else and that they were convinced that the probability of favorable results was closer to 80 percent."

"So in the battle of Linden and his mysterious hedge fund friend against the market consensus, you took Linden and the mystery man for two hundred fifty?"

"Well, I had figured the worst case scenario to be about a hundred grand, but I guess I was wrong."

"I noticed that last week you bought fifteen worth of index puts that were scheduled to expire in two days."

"Yeah, that was just gambling. I've never thought of myself as the type that fights to get back to even, but there's definitely been some of that going on."

"Was the loan to Matt the trigger?"

"I don't know. Maybe. That was a regret that burned. I'm not going to lie. I just couldn't believe I lent him that money. I mean, eighty-two grand. It was just too easy to transfer him that cash online. I didn't have any time to think about it. Matt thought he was doing a cool thing by lying low until he could pay me back, and I guess in a way it *was* a cool thing, but the reality is that it cost me a lot of pain and about six hundred grand."

"Look, the important thing is to move forward. If you don't adjust your risk tolerances to the fact that you're down to a hundred thousand, you're going to go broke.

"You need to transfer your Schwab balances to Bank of America or something. If it sits in the trading account, you're going to trade it to zero. If you still want to play in the ten-thousand dollar tournaments, I'll take up to 50 percent of your action."

Once you lose a healthy sense of risk aversion, it's very hard to get it back.

"I might take you up on that."

"I'll tell you, when we were in L.A., you seemed a bit shakier than normal," I add. "In that pot against Lorenzo, I put you on five-seven without a problem when the last card came down."

Rob commonly makes reads of this type on me, in part because he's better at it and in part because I am prone to massive adrenaline surges that I can't always fully control.

On two occasions, Rob has had me feel his pulse when he was entangled in five-figure pots in online no-limit games. It was hardly north of seventy.

"Losses were heavy at the time. That was a substantial addition to the bankroll."

CHAPTER 9

THE DRINKING
CONTEST

March 24, 2005
Atlantic City

I withdrew $11,000 yesterday, and now I'm standing in front of the same teller hoping to withdraw another $15,000. I feel that withdrawing that kind of cash is an active affront to the teller, as well as everyone else who works for $10 an hour.

I ask the teller if such withdrawals are rare, and she says, "We do them pretty much every day."

"Probably not too many deposits."

"No."

Cash in pocket, I leave for the $2,000 no-limit event at Harrah's. This is part of the World Series of Poker Circuit Tour, a joint venture with ESPN. Walking around Harrah's, I can't help thinking that Atlantic City has an especially high concentration of people who have hit bottom.

Vegas has enough of the California persona that it can put a light touch on desperation. Vegas can part a fool from his money and leave him happy; Atlantic City is all eastern darkness, especially during the week.

Playing a big poker tournament during a weekend feels like a reasonable use of one's time. It's exciting; it's social; it's challenging. Playing in a weekday poker tournament has an entirely different feel. For one, people who play in weekday poker tournaments don't have jobs. This tends to make them somewhat less interesting. Conversation at the table becomes even narrower than usual, usually focused on stories of past successes and rumors about fellow gamblers.

Rob and I both bust out of the tournament in the second hour. We share a cab back to the Borgata, and, after a short wait, take seats in an $80/$160 game. This is undoubtedly the softest game I've ever played in at any limit above $30/$60. Three guys are driving the action. One is a "bounty hunter" from Long Island who flew in for the day on his helicopter. The other is a drunk Argentinean guy who doesn't seem fully cognizant of crucial poker rules, such as the ranking of hands. The wife of the third guy thinks that her husband is at his twentieth Yale reunion; in fact he is on a coke-fueled, sixty-hour poker bender.

I rarely, if ever, drink at the poker table. In big no-limit games, my standard drink order is a hot tea, a bottled water, and a Heineken. I stick with the water and the tea until I take a bad beat or lose an enormous pot, and then I kill the Heineken. There's no strategy behind it; I simply need a beer at such moments. A few weeks ago, a guy seated next to me took a horrendous beat and chugged my beer. Either he didn't know it was mine, or he needed it so badly that he didn't care.

When the waitress comes around, Rob says, "Give me a Grey Goose and soda."

The Argentinean guy cheerfully says, "Give him two," urging Rob to keep up with his pace of two drinks per round.

"Is that a challenge, Sir? I tell you what; we'll order eight drinks each. The first one to finish gets paid $500."

With that, the Argentinean guy peels seven $20 dollar chips from his stack and gives them to the waitress. "Bring us four drinks now and, as soon as those are done, bring out the next four," he says.

"Can I get in on that?" screams the "bounty hunter."

"I'm in, too." This is from the guy on the coke bender. Surely his wife would be proud.

"OK. Fifteen hundred to the winner," Rob confirms with alarming seriousness. Does he realize that in an $80/$160 game, this would almost definitely be a Pyrrhic victory? I'm not sure.

The waitress brings the drinks to the table in two trips. Rob gives the waitress another $160, and says, "Go ahead and bring the second round."

As soon as everything is in place, the "bounty hunter" tips the dealer $20, and says, "We're waiting on your word."

As soon as word is given, all sixteen drinks are downed in under a minute. This is an irrational display of testosterone, as it is obviously going to take at least ten minutes for the second batch of drinks to be delivered.

On completion of his fourth drink, the Yale guy on the coke bender says, "I tell you what, I'll give a grand to anyone who wins a showdown with six-nine."

"I've got a grand on ten-deuce," Rob says.

"I'll put two on deuce-seven," I add.

The five assorted players that round out the table have seats that, in the presence of an open market, might sell for $4,000. One of the guys gets into a fairly heated battle with his wife when he refuses to leave for dinner. Capped pots (four bets) pre-flop, usually rare, are occurring three hands out of four. A deuce on the flop assures that four bets would be thrown in then as well.

The Argentinean guy's wife shows up just as the second batch of drinks arrives. I see a glimmer of doubt flash in his eyes, but after the word "go" is uttered for a second time, he downs his drinks with seemingly impossible speed. Rob is clearly intent on winning this battle, but, along with the other contestants, he has yet to start his fourth glass when the Argentinean finishes.

Upon finishing, the Argentinean guy says, "Good game, friends. I'm not collecting," and, miraculously, stands up from the table. He gives the floor man $100 and says, "Please bag my chips. I'll pick them up later."

Great damage is left in his wake. The eyes of the coke-bender guy seem ready to pop out of their sockets. I hate it for his wife, but I've seen a few cases like that where the eyes stay like that forever.

Rob is passed out over his chips. A vein that I've never seen before is bulging on the left side of his forehead. He's had a total of about seventeen drinks in four hours. I have two options. I can either leave Rob passed out over his chips and hope that he can shake it off tomorrow, or I can drag him from the table, which will make him throw up with high probability. Sensing that the alcohol was probably doing some very serious harm, I call for the floor. "Look, I know this is a weird request," I say, "but I need a wheelchair."

Twenty minutes later, I roll him up to the room. He's passed out but has a contented smile on his face that encourages people to laugh at him. A few people even snap pictures of us as we make our way to the elevators. Rob has a rough half hour in the bathroom once we got to the room, but he seems to be at least partially sentient after I make him down a few bottles of water.

CHAPTER 10

THE TWITCH

March 25, 2005, 12:00 PM
Atlantic City

The next morning, I wake up in worse shape than Rob. He's catastrophically hungover, to be sure, but I have a seemingly permanent twitch near my left eyebrow. I had noticed it before I went to sleep, but I held out hope that it would disappear by morning.

I try working out and going to the spa, but the twitch actually feels worse on my return. I decide to leave Atlantic City immediately, skipping tomorrow's televised $10,000 event. Rob tells me that he's going to stay in the room for the day and recover.

Instead of bothering with train schedules or car rental agencies, I just go downstairs and hop in a cab.

"How much to go to New York?"

"Four hundred."

"One-fifty."

"Two-fifty."

"OK, let's go. Fiftieth Street and Eighth Avenue."

I'm ordering a Blimpie sandwich at a New Jersey rest stop when I think to myself, "I've already paid the cab."

The taxi driver had told me a story about how he had driven a guy to Brooklyn the previous week who had stiffed him on arrival, and he'd asked me to pay him up front. When we stopped forty minutes outside of Atlantic City, my immediate thought had been hitting the men's room. The guy had seemed trustworthy enough.

Alas, when I leave the Blimpie counter and walk outside, I find myself stranded in the middle of New Jersey, minus several thousand dollars in clothes and a laptop that I would pay $5,000 to replace.

I call another cab. The best that I can negotiate is $300, even though the distance is shorter. I get back to my apartment around 4:00 PM. What are you supposed to do with a twitch? I don't know.

I'm pretty sure you're not supposed to play Internet poker, but I don't have enough self-esteem to resist its call. I've discovered that self-respect is a necessary condition for impulse control. Without self-respect, I don't have any impulse control, and my impulse is to play Phil Ivey in heads-up $200/$400 hold 'em on Full Tilt, another of the online card rooms I frequent. Ivey was playing in a limo en route to Atlantic City from New York. I didn't even know that this was technically feasible.

Ivey had knocked me out of the Mirage World Poker Tour event in June of last year. He's one of a handful of players who have convinced me that I have no real shot at becoming one of the game's top players. I've mastered the analytical and mathematical aspects of the game, and I'm reasonably good at reading opponents, but I lack the nimble feel for all the various forms of nervous energy floating around the table that a player like Ivey has. I also lack table presence. A Harvard friend of mine once played in a chess exhibition with Gary Kasparov; he said that when Kasparov stared at him from the other side of the table, he became almost incapable of thought. The Ivey glare is nearly as piercing.

It turns out that playing Internet poker in a limo, while technically feasible, is not advisable. Ivey is disconnecting frequently, at least once every forty hands, and Full Tilt doesn't have disconnect protection, meaning that if your Internet connection fails in the middle of a hand, it is treated as an automatic fold.

All told, I win just over $34,000. I estimate that about $10,000 of this was due to Ivey's bad connection. The rest of the time, I was getting run over by the deck. That's not a bad thing to have happen when you're playing Ivey. He'll tend to pay you off when you have a hand. He's relying on the inevitable long stretches when you're not getting cards; during these times, he'll shut you out of every pot.

Ivey quits the game when his group arrives in Atlantic City. I order some sushi and six Sapporo beers. I eat, drink, and watch *Six Feet Under.* I notice that sometime around my fifth beer, my twitch disappears. I pass out on the couch and wake up at 7:00 AM.

One of the occupational peculiarities of being a poker player is that on any particular day, you don't really have anything to do. You're just kind of winging it, all the time. That's why poker players are always going broke—humans aren't good at that kind of thing. It gives them too many opportunities to fall prey to weakness.

I find myself drawn to action as if by magnetic force. I have always felt this pull, but today it's particularly strong. It screams not just for action but for "the scene," the occasional gathering around big tournaments of the best, the richest, and the most visible poker players.

I throw my DOB kit, two changes of clothes, and a serious amount of cash into a backpack, and then take off downstairs in search of a cab. This time the rate's pretty steep ($400).

I call Rob en route.

"Dude, get this. Sapporo killed my twitch! I'm on my way back to A.C."

"Sweet."

"Are you playing?" I ask.

"Of course."

Once you start playing in big tournaments, you have to keep playing. Continued absence will be perceived as a signal of insolvency. If you have an unconventional playing style, people will be quick to point out that you were a fool all along whose inevitable separation from his money could only be delayed temporarily by luck.

"What's the damage so far this week?" I guess twenty or so.

"About sixteen," Rob says.

"I'll take half your action today."

"No, forget that. How about we trade a third?"

"Yeah, of course."

This means that I'll give Rob one-third of anything I win, and he'll give me one-third of anything he wins. "How's the hangover recovery effort?" I ask.

"Back to 95 percent. I hit the sauna for thirty minutes yesterday and drank probably two gallons of water."

"Nice. I'm a tad hungover from the six-pack of Sapporo."

"That's because you're a lightweight. Hey, I've got to run. Meet me at eleven in front of the tournament sign-up desk."

"Cool. See you there."

CHAPTER 11

TV POKER

March 29, 2005
Atlantic City—Harrah's
$10,000 Tournament—Day 4

I've never played poker on TV before. I'm more than a little nervous about it. I slept a total of four hours last night, and the morning is hellish. They need us there by 11:00 AM. I wake up at 8:30 AM and order room service. By 9:30 AM, room service still hasn't arrived, and I decide that I needed to swim to compose myself.

My goggles aren't working, and the chlorine irritates my eyes to an extent that there's no way I'll be able to wear my contacts for the rest of the day. My glasses had broken just before the trip, so, just before the tournament starts, I have to tie on one of the stems with a small wire. So now I'm about to go on TV with an old pair of glasses that are held together by a visible piece of wire.

I play passive, weak-tight poker for the first forty minutes; the only thing I can think about is how it came to be that I am wearing an embarrassing pair of glasses during my first television appearance. I try to convince myself, to no avail, that it's actually a good thing. You see, the producers don't allow players to wear sunglasses, and my one tic at the poker table is that my eyes tend to visibly enlarge when I get excited. It is a killer tell, and I'm able to conceal it in live play with wraparound sunglasses. The glasses at least provide some level of protection.

At 2:55 PM, toward the end of the first round of play (the blinds are $10,000 and $20,000, and the ante is $2,000), I find myself with a pair of jacks. This is a tough hand to play in tournaments because if you find yourself in a big tangle, your opponent either has two over cards (ace-king, ace-queen, or king-queen) or a higher pair. In the first case, you are a slight favorite; in the second, you are big dog.

The first player to act folds, then Tommy Bo, the chip leader and by far the most aggressive at the table, raises to $60,000. The next player folds, and I instantly raise all in for $160,000. Tommy has ace-nine of diamonds and calls my raise, and, thankfully, the board is free of an ace and supplies only one diamond. My chip stack is now up to a respectable $370,000.

Toward the end of the second hour, an unusual thing happens—two players are eliminated in the same hand. The blinds are now $15,000 and $30,000 with antes of $3,000. Tommy raises to $90,000 under the gun. Luis Viceira, two seats to Tommy's left, goes all in with ace-queen suited for $140,000, and then Lynne Johnston goes all in from the big blind for $520,000 with kings. Tommy had, improbably, picked-up aces. He calls immediately, and his hand holds up.

By the end of that hand, my mood and position in the tournament have improved immeasurably. The chip count is as follows:

Me: 300,000
Tommy Bo: 1.5 million

Ken Lennard: 270,000
Chris Long: 750,000

The tournament payouts are:

First: $780,000
Second: $420,000
Third: $220,000
Fourth: $150,000

The table spars without casualty until the middle of hour four, when blinds are $25,000 and $50,000 with antes of $5,000. At this point, Ken Lennard is severely short-stacked and goes all in for $170,000. I have *A-Q* in the big blind and call his bet. Unfortunately, Ken has *A-K*, so I'm drawing dead to a queen. The board comes *4-4-7* unsuited. The turn brings a *9*. At this point, someone in Ken's camp screams, "Yes," and on cue, a *7* comes. We split the pot.

Ken is not in favor with the poker gods on this day, because two hands later, I go all in for $340,000 with *A-K* unsuited, and he calls from the big blind with *Q-Q*, a slight favorite. The flop comes *K-4-2*, and the turn and river bring *9-9*.

Now we are down to three players. Chris Long and I have roughly equal stacks. Given the chip position and the payout structure, it makes sense for both of us to tread carefully.

Of course, the beauty of tournaments is that if I know that you know that it makes sense to tread carefully, then it makes sense for me to play aggressively to steal your blinds and antes. The science of game theory, my guiding light in poker, assumes that this reasoning continues ad infinitum (if I know that you know that you know that I know ...), and then asks, what is the optimal strategy? Then again, if everyone at the table had infinite calculating ability and perfect game theoretic knowledge, one's probability of winning would be proportionate to the number of chips in front of him. I want to win more often than that. To do it, I have to get in my opponents' heads and figure out where they are stopping along the I-know-that-you-know-that-I-know line.

In this case, my read on Chris is that he isn't going very far down the line at all. He is simply thinking, *I'm going to play cautiously and try to advance to second for the extra $205K.* Given that that's his plan, my best strategy is to play a bit recklessly.

At the end of hour five, I find myself with a pair of kings and reraise Tommy Bo. My hand holds up against ace-jack, and now my stack is nearly twice as large as Chris's. When Chris's all in with fours doesn't hold up against Tommy's ace-seven, I find myself heads up against Tommy for the title, and, more importantly, $1.2 million.

Tommy has me out-stacked four-point-four to one. In the second hand of heads-up play, I reraise all in from the big blind with *Ac-Ks*, and he calls with *9c-9h*. The board comes *3h-3s-4c-5d-Qs*.

They say that only one person leaves the tournament happy. Today, this is emphatically not the case. I have just scored $420,000 after coming to the final table as the short stack in a terrible mental state.

I think about doing the post-game interview without my glasses, but I can't see the camera, so I have to wear them. I'm a bumbling idiot in my post-game interview, partly because I am self-conscious about my glasses, but mostly because I am absurdly wired after playing seven hours of high-intensity poker under the lights and in front of the camera.

After I collect the check, I go up to the room and place an order for two cheeseburgers and four beers. An hour later, these were down, along with four Advil. I go to sleep ten minutes after that (a real pleaser for the digestive system). I am too exhausted and wired to do anything else.

I spend half of the next day at the pool, mostly writing in my journal and talking on the phone. I tell my friends that, improbably, a hellish morning had catapulted me from the short stack to a second-place finish, and, more importantly, $420,000. My weak-tight play, usually a disaster for the short stack, had kept me alive and, when I did make my big moves, I was graced with exceptional luck.

CHAPTER 12

STAYING HOME

March 31, 2005
New York

The wisdom of celebrating victories is usually lost on poker players. Even after a big score, they hunger for action. It's not usual to see someone bemoaning a bad beat for $7,000 after he won $700,000 two weeks before.

Rob and I take a limo home on the day after the tournament. We invite a few friends to Da Silvano and have a generally huge night out, but the next morning Rob breaks the news that he's done celebrating.

"I think I'm going to fly to Vegas tomorrow," Rob says. That would put him in Vegas a day before a $10,000 tournament started at the Rio.

"It's funny. I halfway thought about doing that myself. I think I'm going to chill here, though."

Rob's share of my tournament score came to $140,000, but for him there was no glory involved.

"You have to go. There are probably only going to be two hundred people or so. You'd have a decent chance of two final tables in a row."

"I hate to be the voice of rationality here, but your bankroll now is at, what, two hundred sixty? It's going to cost ten thousand to enter and three thousand for hotels and such. Then the Rio is going to take 6 percent of the prize pool. Not to mention that 80 percent of the money will go to the top few spots, and all that money will be taxed at 40 percent. Plus it's going to be one of the toughest fields of the year."

Rob is in a particularly unfair tax bind in that he won't be able to offset gambling wins with his $500,000 of market losses, since the latter counts as a short-term capital loss, and the former counts as personal income.

"I hear you, but look at what happened in the last week. A cabdriver left you in Atlantic City and stole your luggage. You were so upset about this that you played two-hundred/four-hundred with Phil Ivey, then drank so much beer that you drove your twitch into submission. You woke up the next morning and decided that you were so action-hungry that you had to take your third two-hundred-dollar cab ride in twenty-four hours. I decide to play because you play, and we trade a third, which turns out to be worth a hundred forty. Tell me how I could not go to Vegas after that."

"Well, the alternative is to bask in your good fortune here in the best city in the world. We could go out every night for two weeks and put poker on the shelf for a while."

"Look, I'm going to bask in my good fortune in Vegas, and you know you want to do the same," Rob says.

"Fine. We'll go out tonight, and I'll take a last-minute flight out tomorrow if I have a change of heart."

We order beer and sushi in the apartment at 7:00 PM and never make it out.

The adrenaline rush of the last week has run its course.

Rob takes a 1:00 PM flight the next day. I get a one-hour massage just after he leaves, and I intend to spend the day reading the *New York Times* and otherwise luxuriating.

I spend maybe forty minutes reading the *Times*, and then I take a detailed look at flights to Vegas. There are thirty options, including a couple of good direct flights. I feel the stir and almost book at that moment, but I decide I'll walk to Starbucks and give it some thought on the way.

I sit at the computer with my coffee and again almost book a flight. Out of reflex, I open up a couple of Internet poker sites. There are some interesting games going. I sit at a $150/$300 game on Ultimate Bet and quickly go up $9,000. I open up two $50/$100 no-limit games and sit at those as well. I am up $16,000 across the three tables after less than forty minutes online.

I usually don't take phone calls when I play, but I take a call from Matt.

I say, "I'm playing. What's up?"

He says, "OK, get back to it. Just wanted to tell you that there's an article about you on Poker Pages that you should check out."

While attempting to open the article, I misclick in one of my $50/$100 no-limit games, causing me to raise the pot on the flop when I intend to fold (I have nothing). The guy responds to my raise by going all in, so the misclick costs me $3,400.

The article is flattering but, after I read it, my reigning emotion is still irritation.

I put in a phone call to Rob. He has a connection in Chicago, and there is a chance I can catch him there. I go straight to his voice mail. I wage an internal battle about Vegas. Something in me knows that I should book a flight, but at the same time,

I'm weighed down by the minor logistical problems associated with the trip. I'd have to get cash; I'd have to pack; I'd have to go through detailed security (since I was buying my ticket late); and I'd have to cancel a dinner that I'd planned with a friend for Wednesday night. Rather than thinking about these issues, I decide to just play.

I again go on a mini-run and am up about $19,000 total. One of my $50/$100 no-limit tables has gone heads up. My opponent is extremely aggressive. Both of us have just over $20,000 on the table. I raise to $300 on the button with *As-Qs*, then he reraises to $1,200. Against some players, I consider a fold here, but this opponent has been reraising with high frequency, so I call. The flop comes *Kh-Jd-10s*. Nice. Not only do I flop the nuts, but I do it on a flop that is likely to hit my opponent hard. He bets out $2,400. I call.

The turn comes a *4c*, and he again bets out the pot ($4,800). I put him on a set and raise to $14,400. He calls. I find it odd that he calls because it only leaves him with $3,700, and there is no way he'll be able to fold for $3,700 on the river. I think it's probable that he has a set of kings, and is waiting for the river to stick in the last of his money. The river is a jack, and, sure enough, he puts in his last $3,700. I call—and he turns over *K-J*.

He has just rivered me in a $41,000 pot. His $1,200 reraise pre-flop was a clear mistake. You can reraise with two kings or with five-seven suited but not with king-jack suited because you'll never know where you stand in the hand if you're called. When I raised the pot on the turn, he should have been dead sure that he was beat.

After this enormous pot, I find myself down $1,500. Through a combination of bad luck and hasty play, I go down another $33,000 over the next hour, much of it to the guy who had rivered me with the jack. Perhaps in the spirit of games-manship, he tells me, "If I didn't hit that jack, I was through. That was my whole bankroll!"

I have just one thought: *I have to get to even, and then I'll leave for Vegas*, which was clearly the right decision in the first place. Usually I don't care about getting back to even, but I can't see how I could leave for Vegas down $34,500 when I should have left hours ago without playing at all.

I go on a subtle version of tilt. When making decisions about things like calling versus raising or bluffing versus not bluffing, I always err on the side of action, which is to say that I raise and bluff any time these actions are strategically defensible. It turns out that this is a terrible thing when your opponents are hitting their hands.

I find myself in a vicious cycle in which crazy losses fuel regret about not going to Vegas, which in turn fuel a bad coffee high and some increasingly costly and less subtle forms of tilt. Six hours after the king-jack beat, my total damages are $126,000, and going to Vegas is not a viable option if I want any hope of holding on to my mental health.

I manage to quit at around 9:30 PM. I go to the convenience store closest to my apartment and buy two six-packs. I open a can in the elevator on the way up and open seven more in the apartment.

I wake up the next morning feeling very bad indeed. I con-sider that my only viable option might be to leave for La Guardia immediately and see if I can get on a flight heading to Vegas. It is 7:30 AM. I can get to La Guardia by 8:30 AM, hop on a 9:30 AM flight, get there by 11:30 AM local time, and then head straight to the Rio. Again the contemplation of the minor difficulties associated with this course keeps me from executing it. I find myself sulking over eggs and coffee at my local diner.

How does one go about the day in such circumstances? Rarely has it been so plain to me that one course of action is better than another. There is simply no conceivable case as to how staying in New York is the better option for me. Usually there's some kind of straw to grab onto in defense of the chosen option. Maybe you meet a girl that you might be interested in, or you have a great idea. Here, there was nothing.

I find myself retracing steps in time to see where exactly I have gone wrong. Given the sensitive dependence of life to initial conditions, what initial condition, specifically, would I alter? The main candidates are Matt's phone call, the $3,400 misclick, the jack on the river, and the "that was my whole bankroll" comment, but there are, of course, a hundred other events and thoughts, the alteration of which would have produced a different outcome.

In the movie *Waking Life*, the main character asks, "Where are you taking me?"

The driver replies, "Just a spot that will determine the rest of your life."

I have a brain that should never get started along this path. My fine attunement to the sensitivities of life, to small changes coupled with the dizzying array of possibilities that such a contemplation suggests, means that once I get started thinking along these lines, I can't stop.

After breakfast, I do a very stupid thing. I take the last $21,000 that I have on Neteller and deposit it at Ultimate Bet. I find myself against the very same opponent who I had been heads up against the night before. He immediately starts needling me in the chat box: "DUDE, YOU WERE ON CRAZY TILT LAST NIGHT."

(I don't think it was that bad.) "I'M EIGHTEEN. HOW OLD ARE YOU? I WILL USE YOUR MISTAKES AGAINST YOU. THERE'S NO OTHER CHOICE."

He plays as poorly as before, but his luck has not run out, and my $21,000 is on his side of the table in less than an hour.

At this point, I realize that I have to go to Vegas. Otherwise, I'll continue to think about how I found myself in this weird alternate universe where my decision not to go to Vegas cost me $147,000 and some measure of mental health. I get on Expedia and book a flight leaving at 8:20 PM that night.

CHAPTER 13

SITTING OUT

April 2, 2005
Vegas—Mirage

The trip to Vegas taunts me by being utterly without hassle. I write myself little edicts during the flight like, "Damage limitation in bad times is one of the essential skills."

I keep trying to put a positive spin on things, but my mind won't let me. The last two weeks had been good, the last two days had been bad; shouldn't I be able to take the longer view?

I get to the Rio around midnight, and day one of the tournament is still going. Rob doesn't seem surprised to see me. I'm not sure if anything truly surprises Rob. That's a good mindset to have for poker. It keeps one from being overwhelmed by the confluence of chance factors that work together to determine one's reality at any given time.

Antoine comes up to me while I'm on the rail. "I busted two hours ago," he says. "Set over set. Congrats on the big finish in A.C. What was it, four-forty?"

Actually, I want to say, it was two-thirds of that, or one hundred fifty-four thousand after tax, and I've already lost most of that in seven hours of Internet poker. Instead, I go with, "Yeah. Rob had a third of it.

"Are you playing cash games tonight? I'm going to head over to the Bellagio in a bit," I say. This was not really in the plans. I just kind of say it to extricate myself from the conversation. Now that I've said it, though, I realize that it's what I need to do.

"You taking off now?" The tone in his voice indicates that I don't look like I'm in the state for it. "There's a chance I'll see you over there tonight. I'm feeling pretty burnt out at the moment. For sure I'll see you over there tomorrow."

I hit the ATM and take out $3,000 using three ATM cards, and then I head to the Bellagio. One of the problems with running bad is that you're too focused on the past to make plans. The lack of plans usually means that you give way to impulse. Impulse and poker are not good bedfellows.

Since the jack on the river a day and a half ago, my reigning impulse has been to play bigger and faster in an attempt to get even. Fortunately, I'm saved from doing that tonight by the fact that I don't have cash on me aside from that supplied by the ATM. I sit down at a $10/20 no-limit game with all $3,000.

On the third hand of the night, four players limp in (match the blinds, but don't raise) for twenty; then I raise to $120 from the button with *6s-4s*. There is no intellectual justification for this. I just want action. The small blind raises to $460, and one of the early limpers calls, declaring his small pair and his incompetence. When it gets around to me, I have a couple of quick thoughts. The first is that, although the initial $120 raise was not clearly a bad play, calling an additional $340 certainly would be. The second is that I am surely going to have to call the $340.

The flop comes *3s-9d-10c*. The small blind bets out $600, and the early limper folds. As the action comes to me, I have a clear vision of my strategy. I'll call the $600; then I'll represent a set on the turn. The turn comes *2h*. The small blind checks; I bet $700. I have him at 30 percent aces, 50 percent kings, and 20 percent queens.

He calls the $700. OK, not that surprising. The river comes *2c*. Perfect. He checks again. I say, "I'm all in."

He sighs and says, "How much is it?"

"Thirteen ten," I say.

"OK," he says, "I call." He turns over *A-A*.

"Nice hand," I say.

One of the players asks if he can see my hand, a terrible breach of etiquette. The dealer turns over my six-four of spades. I have no choice but to leave the table. I am out of cash.

Calling a reraise pre-flop with a drawing hand and then representing a set when you miss is a completely standard strategy. My mistake in the hand had been that, first, I'd called too big a raise with too weak a starting hand, and, second, I'd "represented" a set against a player who I had no read on. He might not have realized that I was representing a set, or he might have just been the type that couldn't fold an over-pair even when he's fairly certain he's beat. In short, it was my third hand of the night; he didn't know me, I didn't know him.

What sticks with me about the hand is that I didn't for a second consider the question, "What is the best play here?" I instead focused on the strategy that involved the heaviest action and went to work justifying that play. That's more or less the definition of tilt.

I book a ticket to Maui for Thursday when I get back to the hotel room. It seems like the obvious thing to do. I just couldn't be around poker right then.

When I get back to the Rio, the players are packing up their chips for the night. "Rob, what's the count?"

He tells me $24,500. That would be a bit north of average.

"Man, I came here to watch, but I can't be around poker right now. I'm taking off tomorrow."

"You're looking pretty shitty. You're going to have to fill me in later."

I stay in Maui for eight days. I read six books and don't play a single hand of poker.

CHAPTER 14

THE EARLY
EVENTS

June 8, 2005
Vegas—Rio

In 2004, ESPN filmed fourteen events at the World Series of Poker. A college kid can win a $200 satellite, have a good day, and then find himself playing on TV. A month later, he could walk in any poker room in the United States, and 60 percent of the people there will know his name.

The World Series of Poker, especially the $10,000 main event, is the primary annual gathering spot for poker players across the world. Failure to attend is considered an admission of financial ruin. My gauge of a player's bankroll comes primarily from the WSOP. If a player is not solvent enough to afford the main event, he is advised to play at least one or two smaller but highly visible events such as the $1,000 no-limit hold 'em with rebuys. This will show that he or she is not broke; poker is one of the few fields of endeavor where this is an exalted status.

In poker, everyone finds it important to project a winning persona, and nowhere is this truer than at the World Series of Poker. After considering the rake, perhaps 90 percent of poker players are long-term losers, yet I can count on one hand the number of players that have confessed to being long-term losers. Among Internet players, this self-denial is taken to another level; nearly every Internet player you meet claims to have made an astronomical sum playing Internet poker. This doesn't square well with the fact that Party Poker's revenues in 2004 were $600 million.

My plan is to play in twenty-three tournaments with entry fees of $1,500 or greater this World Series. Playing in such tournaments is, in many ways, irrational. For one, these tournaments commonly have 800 players or more, and one player usually takes home 40 percent of the prize pool. That makes for quite a lot of variance. In a high buy-in tournament, the best poker player in the world might be three times more likely than the average player to win.

The luck element in tournaments is so strong that even the worst player has some chance; I once played in a $3,000 Omaha tournament at Bellagio (one hundred forty players) in which the guy who won had never played Omaha before and was only vaguely aware of the rules.

Cash game players often adopt the same tax-planning strategies as bellmen and bartenders. The tournament player does not have that luxury. Tournament wins are well documented, and the player is advised to report them. Most players are, in effect, entering a tournament with after-tax money, and then being paid out in taxable money.

When cash game players finds themselves all in with ace-king suited against a pair of queens pre-flop, they know that their chances are roughly fifty-fifty. They might win or lose that particular hand, but they can assume that luck will not have a big influence on their long-term results. They might play twenty such hands over the course of the year; if they are very unlucky, they might win seven and lose thirteen.

It is not unusual for a player who typically plays $10/$20 no-limit to enter a $3,000 tournament, do well, and then suddenly take a bad beat near the end that is worth $60,000 in expected value terms. In the end stages of a tournament, all-in pre-flop moves are common, and when they meet resistance, the winner is usually determined primarily by luck.

In some games, like chess, the rules are clear, and serious disputes rarely occur in competitive play. In poker, this is not the case. For one, the rules with respect to proper procedure differ by card room location. When conflict arises, the dealer and the floor person are left with a lot of discretion. This can bring about some unusual and sometimes heated situations.

Late in the $3,000 no-limit tournament, I find myself facing a highly unusual situation. With blinds of $500 and $1,000 and antes of $100, I'm dealt *9h-10h* in the big blind. The worst player at the table raises it to $3,000 from the button. Against a better player, I'd fold in that spot, but I think I can bust this guy if I hit my hand. The flop comes *K-3-4* (two hearts). I check; he bets $4,000; I call. The turn comes a blank (*8s*). I check; he checks. When the river brings *Ac*, I pat the table (indicating a check), and I'm sure that I see him do the same thing, so I turn my hand over.

With that, he looks at the dealer and says, "I didn't check."

I'm so mystified by this that I don't even bother with an argument. The dealer clearly had not been paying full attention, so after I sit in silence for a second, he yells out, "Floor!"

The floor person's ruling is that, since no one can confirm that my opponent did in fact check, he will be allowed the opportunity to bet, even though he has seen my cards.

With that ruling, my opponent says, confidently, "I'm all in," meaning a bet of 17,000 chips into a 15,500 chip pot.

"OK," I think to myself, "This is poker."

I rarely spend more than two minutes coming to a decision, but in this case I spend a lot of time examining the guy before a clock is called.

*   *   *   *

Reflecting on this episode later, I would consider the fact that it was the perfect illustration of why a computer could never become the best poker player in the world in the way that Deep Blue became the best player in chess. The academic discipline of game theory provides the basis for all poker-playing software. Game theory is based on the idea that if two players are involved in a strategic game, both players are reasoning something like, *I think that he thinks that I think X, therefore I should do this.* Game theory assumes that since both players are thinking in this fashion, then the optimal strategy for each player is to choose his or her best option, given that the other player is carrying out the I-think-that-he-thinks-that-I-think logic to the infinite degree. Real poker players know that their opponents don't think about things to the infinite degree; they think about things to the nth degree, and it is left to the players' judgment to determine what "n" is. Only then can they respond in such a way as to extract the maximum amount from their opponent.

I spend a total of eight minutes contemplating whether or not I should call. There are only 13 of 169 possible starting hands that I could beat at this point, and most of those are poor hands such as deuce-seven that are usually thrown away pre-flop. Yet, the glaring fact is that, if he could beat ten high, why would he call the floor? Just check. Hand's over. You win.

From a game theory perspective, the best play is for your opponent to go all in if he can beat ten high. It's a clear-cut dominant strategy; in the worst case, you win what is in the pot (the same outcome as checking), but if there is any chance at all that your opponent will put you on a bluff, he will call, and you will win those chips as well. Couple his strategic situation with the fact that there are very few plausible starting hands that lose to ten high in a showdown, and you have a seemingly clear-cut fold.

An unethical opponent could in fact use something like this as a move, making you think that, somehow, he can't beat ten high (or some other bad hand), and therefore inducing you to call in an unlikely spot.

*   *   *   *

In the end, poker is about feel, and my feel was that my opponent was coming at this from the simplest possible strategic perspective: *I can't beat ten high. If I check, I'll lose, so I'll bet.* There's no analytical basis for this. It's a read, pure and simple, based on my view of my opponent's strategic depth, intelligence, and emotional state. And as it turns out, it was right. I decide to call. He turns over *6h-7h.*

Three hours later, with blinds of $1,000/$2,000 and an ante of $300, I raise to $8,000 from the button with *As-9s.* Erick Lindgren calls from the big blind. The flop comes *9h-Jh-Jd.* Erik checks; I bet $16,000. Then Lindgren says, "I'll put you all in." It'll cost me a little more than nineteen thousand to call.

It's a tough decision. Erik could make this play with a wide range of hands. My top candidate for his holding is king-queen, giving him two over cards and a gut shot straight draw. Second most likely is a flush draw with one or possibly two over cards, and other contenders are ace-jack, king-jack, or queen-jack. A pocket pair is a small possibility. He might also make this play with a hand such as ace-ten that missed the flop entirely. The top players tend to be quite aggressive because aggressive play always leaves opponents guessing in this manner. Conservative players have a tighter range of possible holdings in any given post-flop situation and are therefore easier to read.

I spend a few minutes mulling over this decision. I try to always maintain a bias toward folding when faced with big bets or raises. Subconsciously, you're always looking for a reason to call, because calling resolves uncertainty, and the mind abhors uncertainty. If you call, you might lose, but at least you *know.* If you fold, you always have to wonder, "Did they really have it?" I've heard people who faced a big bet on the river say, "I can't call this. Wait, I've got to call."

In the end, I decide that his range of possible holdings here is simply too wide for me to consider folding. He turns up *A-A.* I'm drawing to two outs, and they don't hit.

Erik had played this beautifully. The ratio of hands that I'd raise with on the button to those that I'd call a reraise with was very high, so Erik had figured that he'd make more money by just calling and then check-raising. He knows that in a lot of cases, I'll raise with marginal hands on the button, and then bet out on the flop after he checks, even if the flop misses my hand completely. As it turns out, Erik had met the best of possible worlds: I hit enough of the flop that I'd call his raise, but not so much of it that I was a favorite over his hand.

CHAPTER 15

THE MAIN EVENT

July 8, 2005
Vegas—Harrah's
World Series of Poker—Day 1

There was an early consensus that the main event would sell out all 6,600 seats a month before the tournament began. These early prognostications proved wrong—the event started yesterday with 5,619 players. Despite the fact that Harrah's had set up what must be the biggest tournament room in the history of poker for the event, players had to be split up into three separate starting days. Both Rob and I drew Day Two.

We had grown to hate the Rio over the past six weeks. It's not that it was a bad venue; it was just a bit impersonal, and, for Rob and me, it had no history extending beyond the current year, which had been, for us, spectacularly unsuccessful and not particularly fun or memorable.

"It's incredible how much you can lose during a bad World Series," Rob sums up as we eat breakfast.

"Yeah, in tournaments, we pretty much lost the maximum."

I had played thirty events. Rob had played twenty-seven. We had a cumulative total of four cashes, and all four of those had been under $5,000.

"What was your cash game total?" Rob asks, knowing that I usually kept good track of such things.

"Twenty-seven hours. Plus eighteen hundred," I say.

Twenty-seven hours was not a lot of play over six weeks. The tournaments burned me out. We got so caught up in the whole bracelet-TV-glory thing that we forgot that winning money should be a favored objective.

"I'm not 100 percent sure, but I think I'm around minus fourteen thousand. That day of fifty-one hundred no-limit killed me. I was up seven outside of that," I tell him.

I have mentally lost track of Rob's overall financial picture, but I am sure that it isn't good. Given that we are about to start playing in a $10,000, 5,600-person event, it doesn't seem like a good time to ask him.

"How much are we trading in this thing?" I ask.

"I don't know. Thirty." Rob says.

"OK, sounds good."

Rob would get 30 percent of my winnings, and I would get 30 percent of his. In a tournament with 5,600 players, it would be wise to find many different players that you respect and trust, and trade small pieces with each of them. I had intended to do this, but I'd been too lazy to coordinate it.

As Rob and I walk to the tournament area, I mention to him that, during the six weeks we'd been in Vegas, I had somehow managed to spend a bit more than $350 a day outside of poker.

"How in the hell did you do that?"

"One-sixty a day for hotel, forty a day for rental car, one-fifty a day on random shit. That doesn't include rent in New York, health insurance, or any of my monthly bills."

We usually don't talk about this stuff, but it weighs heavily on my mind. It means that, when coupled with my poker losses, I had shelled out a bit more than $180,000 in six weeks.

"Shit, I haven't even looked at my expenses. I've got to be north of one-fifty a day on random shit. When a guy draws out on you to take a fifteen grand pot, it's kind of hard to sweat fifteen bucks for a vodka cranberry. Know what I mean?"

I take that as a rhetorical question. Of course I know what he means. How do you keep spending in perspective while gambling large portions of your wealth on a daily basis? I'll let you know when I meet someone who's figured it out.

Harrah's has it set up so that to get to the tournament area, you have to walk through the WSOP Lifestyle Show. This includes every line of poker-related business, including both well-established ones (such as Party Poker.com, with a market capitalization of $6 billion) and newly founded hopefuls.

Most of the players in the 2005 main event are playing in their first-ever $10,000 tournament. The reigning vibe is that the $10,000 wasn't a big deal. The prize pool of the tournament is nearly $60 million, and most of that will be paid to the top finishers. This means that towards the end of the tournament, it's entirely possible to take a bad beat worth a million or two.

I'm not sure what to think of my table. I don't recognize anyone. Two guys to my right are engaged in a conversation about the standard deviation of their respective hourly win rates on the PartyPoker $30/$60 hold 'em game. There's a sensitive social dynamic to a poker game, and these guys are so loud and so animated that there's a good chance they'll cause the rest of the table to retreat into silence.

Before the director announces, "Shuffle up and deal," someone comes up to sing the national anthem. The guy to my right stays in his seat. Afterward, he says, "What the fuck are they doing? That was a joke."

"Agreed," I say. This seems to give me an instant rapport with a guy who looks like he doesn't develop an instant rapport with very many people.

"I'm Tariq," he says. I quickly learn that he is an Iraqi psychotherapist living in Santa Cruz. He doesn't play much poker, but he decided he should play this tournament because it was a "cultural event." Tariq was surely, as they say, "dead money," but the Breguet watch on his wrist indicates to me that he can afford to be dead money if he wants to.

"See those two," he whispers to me, "they use their standard deviation as a way to exercise control. It symbolizes for them the control they have over themselves and over other people."

I'm nodding and trying to figure out why he's telling me this.

"Their faces are the texture of aged cheese from gambling and smoking, and yet they are in control. It's so American, isn't it?"

"What is American?"

"The way they are so pleased with themselves for wasting their lives in front of a computer. Money is the only recompense they receive for an empty cultural stock. It is sick."

Tariq is a terrible card player. He has a trait shared by many beginning players in that he won't bet his good hands for fear that, if he does, his opponents will fold. This fear induces him to wait for others to bet his hands for him. Of course, this is the

World Series, so more often than not his opponents decline to bet until they have outdrawn him.

On two different occasions, Tariq flops a set in a multi-way pot and slow plays it, only to be outdrawn on the turn by a flush in one instance and a straight in the other. In both cases, all the money goes in on the turn, and the board pairs on the river, giving Tariq a winning full house.

Tariq and I both make it to the dinner break. The two of us have dinner at a seafood restaurant in the Rio.

I receive a text message from Rob at the start of the dinner break that says, "Still in—24,000 chips. Headache. Going for a run."

The tournament room is packed with players and spectators, and the halls outside the room are full of cigarette smoke. In such an environment, an adrenaline high can easily turn against you. This seems to have happened to Rob. Going for a run is surely a good idea, though I have no clue as to how he plans to fit it into the ninety-minute break.

July 9, 2005
Vegas—Harrah's
World Series of Poker—Day 2

On day two, I land at a table with two pros, one retired guy who travels the tournament circuit, and six weak-tight Internet qualifiers who seem to be satisfied with making it to day two and feel no urgent need to accumulate chips. I run my stack up to 192,000 tournament chips without ever putting it in serious jeopardy.

At around 2:00 AM, on the first hand of the last level of day two, the second guy to act pre-flop shoves his hand toward the dealer carelessly and causes one of his cards to flip over. When this happens, the dealer simply exposes that card to the table, and the hand continues. The exposed card is the six of hearts.

I open with a raise to 7,000 from the button with *Qh-Kh*. The table chip leader calls from the big blind. The flop comes *Qd-Kd-6c*. The chip leader immediately bets out 17,000 chips. I raise to 50,000. He thinks for a while, and then says, "I'm all in."

I run through the possibilities. The exposed six makes his probability of having a set of sixes two-thirds less likely than it otherwise would be. It is possible, but extremely, unlikely that he would decline to reraise pre-flop with pocket kings or queens against a fellow big stack.

Given that a six is exposed and given that I hold a king and a queen, the probability of him making a set given that he has a pair is reduced from one eighth to one twenty-fourth. Coupling this with the fact that it is unlikely that he has either a pair of kings or queens, I come to the conclusion that he is most likely on a very strong draw. My top candidates for his holding are jack-ten of diamonds, ace-ten of diamonds, and ace-jack of diamonds. Given the range of hands he is capable of playing, ace-six of diamonds is possible but unlikely.

In the absence of the exposed six, I would fold this hand. A fold leaves me with 135,000 chips going into day three, which is slightly better than average chip position. Making it to day three also means making it into the money, but I'm not particularly concerned about that—I'm more concerned about maximizing my tournament equity, which effectively means maximizing my chances of making it deep in the tournament.

The exposed six reduces the number of possible starting hands from 1,081 to 1,035 and decreases the number of hands that strongly dominate me given this board from five (Kc-Ks,

Qc-Qs, 6h-6d, 6h-6s, and 6d-6s) to three (Kc-Ks, Qc-Qs, and 6d-6s). Several drawing hands, especially jack-ten of diamonds, are a favorite over me given this flop, but the number of chips in the pot mandates a call in this situation.

After five minutes, one of the players at my table calls the clock on me. This means that I have to make my decision in sixty seconds or my hand will be dead.

The exposed six changed the math just enough that I have to call. Needless to say, he turns over the nightmare hand of *6d-6s*, and the turn and river come *2c-2h*.

Poker, at one point, had taught me to accept chance. Poker players are too narcissistic and self-absorbed to take nonmaterial losses well, but when they are in stride, they are masters at accepting material losses in cards and in life. Poker players are often unusually composed in the face of extreme losses. "What, I lost my house in a hurricane? Bad beat."

At one point in my life, poker had kept me from replaying unfortunate events over and over again in my head. Now I'm in the habit again, and the events I play back are of the most trivial sort. With respect to poker, I still feel like I'm in some weird alternate universe that I switched into after the phone call with Matt and the king-jack beat.

CHAPTER 16

RUNNING BAD

July 18, 2005
Vegas—Harrah's

"Guys, I'm thinking about taking a job," I say.

"Are you serious?" Matt asks. "Why?"

"I'm just worried that this isn't going anywhere. Poker has occupied most of my mental energy for four years. I'm quickly becoming a boring person," I say.

"You'll be boring if you quit poker." Matt says. "What are you going to do?"

"This Iraqi guy at the main event set me up with his cousin in Boston. It's finance. I'd work for a quant-oriented mutual fund at Putnam."

With this career move, I'd risk trading one life defined by trivialities for another.

Matt asks, "Are you broke?"

"No, but I've been running bad since A.C.," I say.

"I didn't think you ran bad," Matt says.

"I'm not playing poorly, but these days, I only get fired up about the bigger games and tournaments. If that's all you play, it's hard to post good results."

We play a zero-sum game with a huge deadweight loss in the form of rakes and dealer tokes. Add to this the unfavorable tax treatment accorded poker players, extremely high living expenses, and the extraordinary variance that's inherent in poker, and you find that the probability of running bad is extremely high. By implication, anyone who has played for a long time without going broke is one hell of a poker player.

"It's no secret that I'm more or less broke, but the way I look at it is that you'd have to be crazy to leave poker now. There's never been so much easy money," Matt says.

Matt had given me an update on his finances yesterday. He's paid off all but $22,000 of his debt to Rob and will almost surely repay that in the near future. He has $8,000 at E*Trade, $11,000 on online poker sites, and a car that he could sell for $25,000 or so.

"Were you not at the main event last week? We were playing with idiots," Rob says.

"Rob, you've got the same problem I do. You only want to play the big games and the big events. You made fourteen thousand playing ten/twenty no-limit. Then you lost twenty-one grand playing fifty/one hundred no-limit. That's been the story of our lives," I say.

"You guys didn't have the best game selection during the Series," Matt says. "I mean, each of you spent six grand on Stud Hi-Lo events. Rob, you hardly know how to play Stud Hi-Lo, and, Raf, I'm sorry, but you're no Ted Forrest."

"For sure, the Stud Hi-Lo stuff was a little out of hand," Rob says. "The way I look at it is that the World Series was kind of a last hurrah. From here on, it's back to the grind."

"Rob," I say, "you've never done the grind."

Truthfully, he doesn't need to. He's good enough to beat almost any game he decides to sit in. Like many before him, though, his quest for action drives him towards bigger and bigger stakes, and games at the highest stakes are among the few games that Rob can't beat.

"When would you start?" Rob asks.

"We're talking about September fifteenth."

"Make me a promise then. Tell me you'll go to L.A. with us for a last hurrah."

Rob is referring to the $5,000 World Poker Tour event in L.A. in early September.

"Of course, I'll be there. I'm not going to quit the big tournaments just because I'm taking a job. I'm just trying to balance things out a little."

In truth, I doubt balance is possible. Quitting full stop is probably the intelligent option, but it's not a very credible one.

I e-mail Tariq about L.A. two weeks before the tournament. He writes back, "I'm definitely in. Don't get a place—I'm going to book a suite for the group at the Le Méridien."

CHAPTER 17

THE LAST HURRAH

September 10, 2005
L.A.—The Bicycle Club
L.A. WPT—Day 1

"How many sign-ups do they have so far?" I ask.

"Seven hundred and something," Rob says.

"Wow. Which day do you start on?"

"Day two. We'll all be day two. You had to get here early for day one."

"When I called yesterday, they said that almost everyone would start on day one. Now you're telling me that half the field is going to start tomorrow?"

"I've told you before," Rob says. "Dealing with tournament organizers is like dealing with the cable guy ... 'What, you'll be there sometime between 10:00 AM and 4:00 PM? No problem! I'll stay home all day. Whatever works for *you*.'"

"If we didn't have such a vicious need for action, I'm sure they couldn't toy around with us so easily," Matt adds.

Indeed, last year, many of the participants were forced to play in outdoor tents in ninety-five-degree heat on day one, and the numbers suggest that a large fraction of these players returned for this year's event.

Day 2

The tournament proves to be a huge disappointment. Tariq learns about the perils of ace-queen when he calls a reraise with it, then loses all his chips to kings when the board comes queen-two-three rainbow. Matt goes out in hour three when his flopped two pair loses to a set, Rob goes out in hour four when his opponent's flush draw hits on the river, and I go out in hour five with pre-flop kings against aces.

Our last poker game together is of the old-school variety. Back at the hotel, we order room service and take out a deck of cards, killing all chances of us making it out.

"This might be the last game we play in a while," Rob says.

"We need to make it a good one," I say. "Bullshit?"

"It's on," Rob says.

"What are we playing for?" Matt asks.

"Money's no good among friends," I say. "We're playing for punishments."

"Break out the 151. Ten-capper," Rob says.

"I tell you what: we'll make it a vodka seven-capper. The loser has to take a cab to Hustler and play three/six limit until 6:00 AM. If we check on him, and he's not there, he loses his car for two weeks. Tariq, that work for you?"

"Sure."

A player would have to take a shot if he called "bullshit" on someone when he had the goods or if someone called bullshit on him and he didn't have the goods. A seven-capper means that the first person to do seven shots is the loser.

I'm in the toughest position—directly to Rob's right. On the first hand, he tells me, "You know my sole objective is to maximize the probability of you playing at Hustler." Given this game dynamic, it's not surprising that we find ourselves at midnight with a score of: Me, six shots; Rob, six shots; Tariq, three shots; and Matt, two shots.

On the last hand of the night, Matt looks at me confidently and says, "Four kings with a six."

I had started this hand with two kings and then passed it to Rob, who had declared, "three kings with a four."

Tariq had declared safely, "Three kings with a five."

My read on Matt is that he had indeed picked up the fourth king, so I accept his hand.

I don't look at the hand for a second. I want to think over my strategy with Rob. One strategy would be to say, "Four kings with a seven," without redrawing or looking at my cards. In all probability, Rob has read Matt for four kings just as I have. The fifth card is, of course, more likely to be above seven than below seven.

I decide to look and draw a card, mainly because I have visions of drawing a high card and trapping Rob. I had been given four kings and a seven. I draw a three.

"Four kings with a nine," I say.

"Really, a nine," Rob says. "That's interesting, because it kind of looks like you were trying to trap me and missed. Why not just look at the cards and declare four kings with an eight? You got a little greedy, didn't you?" Rob turns to Tariq and says, "Nine's kind of interesting, right? He could have said queen, then if I accept, I have to tell you ace, and you send me packing for the Hustler." Rob turns to me again. "Why not go with queen? You didn't think you could lie to me?"

All of this is for show. I don't know how he picks up on it. I rarely do. We look at each other blank-faced for a moment; then I look at the other two and say, "Who wants to call my cab?"

Rob pours two shots and stands up. He looks at Tariq and Matt and says, "Boys, it's been a pleasure." He hands me a glass. "I'm going to take a shot with this man, and then we're going to play some three/six. We'll see you in the morning."

Solution to Logic Problem:

First note that since one of the numbers equals the sum of the other two, then each logician knows that his number must be either the sum of the two numbers he sees or the difference.

I will first go over why the solution is the solution, then I'll go over how one would go about getting the answer.

(20, 30) is a unique solution to the problem.

To see why (20, 30) is the solution, note how the logicians would reason given that Logician One has fifty written on his head:

1. Logician One, first time around: I see twenty and thirty. I am either the sum or the difference; I could be ten or fifty. I cannot deduce anything at this point.

2. Logician Two, first time around: I see fifty and thirty. I can be twenty or eighty. I cannot deduce anything at this point.

3. Logician Three, first time around: I see twenty and fifty. I can be thirty or seventy. I cannot deduce anything at this point.

4. Logician One, second time around: I am either ten or fifty. If I were ten, then Logician Three would have reasoned as follows: "I see ten and twenty. I cannot be ten, since my number must be unique, so I must be thirty." Since Logician Three was not able to conclude that his number was thirty, my number cannot be ten—it must be fifty.

A complete solution method to the problem would give the answer and would show that the answer is unique.

The first thing to note is that Logician One would speak only if the two numbers he or she sees are equal. Since Logician One knows that his number is a positive integer (and thus can't be zero), if the two numbers he saw were equal, he'd know that he was the sum. Thus, Logician One would speak only if the numbers for One, Two, and Three corresponded to all positive multiples of the vector $(2,1,1)$.

The solution method gets trickier from here.

Logician Two likewise would speak if the two numbers he saw were identical. Thus, he would speak if the numbers for One, Two, and Three correspond to all positive multiples of the vector $(1,2,1)$.

Logician Two gleans additional information from the fact that Logician One doesn't speak. Specifically, if Logician Two sees that Logician One's number is twice Logician Three's number, he would know that his number must be the sum rather than the difference. Thus, Logician Two would speak if the numbers for Logicians One, Two, and Three correspond to all positive multiples of the vector $(2,3,1)$. The reason for this is that Logician Two knows that the vector $(2,1,1)$ is impossible, since Logician One would have spoken if he saw that Logician Two and Three had identical numbers.

Based on similar reason, Logician Three would speak if the numbers for One, Two, and Three corresponded to positive multiples of the vectors:

a. (1,1,2). If he sees two identical numbers, he knows he is the sum, since he can't be zero.

b. (2,1,3). If he sees (2,1,X), he knows he is 3, since Logician One would have spoken if he had seen that Logician Two and Three had the same number. In other words, the action would never get around to Logician Three in the (2,1,1) case because if Logician One sees (X,1,1), he knows that his number is 2.

c. (1,2,3). If he sees (1,2,X), he knows he is 3, since Logician Two would have spoken in the (1,2,1) case.

d. (2,3,5). If he sees (2,3,X), he knows he is 5, since Logician Two would have spoken in the (2,3,1) case. Recall that Logician Two speaks in the (2,3,1) case because he recognizes that Logician One would have spoken in the (2,1,1) case. The fact that Logician One doesn't speak allows Two to know that if he sees (2,X,1), then his number is 3. Likewise, the fact that Logician Two doesn't speak allows Three to conclude that if he sees (2,3,X), his number is 5, since if it were (2,3,1), Logician Two would have known his number.

The second time around, Logician One would speak if the numbers for One, Two, and Three corresponded to positive multiples of the vectors:

a. (3,2,1). If he sees (X,2,1), he knows that he can't be 1, since Logician Two would have spoken in the (1,2,1) case.

b. (4,3,1). If he sees (x,3,1), he knows, he knows he can't be 2, since Logician Two would have spoken in the (2,3,1) case.

c. (3,1,2). If he sees (x,1,2), he knows he can't be 1, since Logician Three would have spoken in the (1,1,2) case.

d. (4,1,3). If he sees (x,1,3), he knows he can't be 2, since Logician Three would have spoken in the (2,1,3) case.

e. (5,2,3). If he sees, (x,2,3), he knows he can't be 1, since Logician Three would have spoken in the (1,2,3) case.

f. (8,3,5). If he sees, (x,3,5), he knows he can't be 2, since Logician Three would have spoken in the (2,3,5) case.

Given that Logician One knows that his number is 50 on the second time around, (5,2,3) is the only vector that works. Therefore, the other two numbers must be 20 and 30.

978-1-58348-471-5
1-58348-471-X

Lightning Source UK Ltd.
Milton Keynes UK
10 March 2010

151197UK00001B/51/P